DUDLEY PUBLIC LIBRARIES

KGHt.
DW.

The loan of this book may be renewed if not required by other readers, by contacting the Library from which it was borrowed.

CP/494

Published by Accent Press Ltd – 2006
ISBN 1905170300

The Quick Reads project in Wales is a joint venture between the Basic
Skills Agency and the Welsh Books Council. Titles are funded
through the Basic Skills Agency as part of the National Basic Skills
Strategy for Wales on behalf of the Welsh Assembly Government.

Printed and bound in the UK by
Cox & Wyman Ltd, Reading, Berkshire

Cover Design by Emma Barnes

CHAPTER ONE

I WOKE WITH A start, not knowing where I was. And with that came a moment of panic. But I wasn't pinned to the bed by an intruder, simply by a twisted-up sheet. It was a hot night. It had been a hot evening, the late summer sun seeping into the flat and turning the air thick with dust and scent. I'd tried leaving the windows open, but the steady drone of late evening traffic had forced me to shut them and sweat it out as best I could.

I wasn't sure what had woken me, but even as I untangled my limbs from the fabric and took in the strange surroundings, it began again, a low buzzing sound. That was it. That was where I was. At my sister's flat in Cardiff. And something was going bump in the night.

'Crisis!' Ffion had said cheerfully a week ago. She was phoning because her nanny had let her down, and she had to go to New York for a week. Not leading the high life myself, I knew as much about nannies as I did about rocket science, but I knew she shared her nanny with

1

a couple who lived nearby. They had two toddlers and the mother only worked mornings, which fitted perfectly with Ffion's rather less routine lifestyle, because the nanny was then free for after-school and overnight stints. But not this time, it seemed.

'My nanny's going to have her wisdom teeth out,' Ffion explained, 'so she's got to go into hospital.' I knew how hard it was trying to run your life as a working single mum. Ffion had been doing it since Emily was three, with varying disasters along the way. It was only in the last couple of years that she'd been able to afford the luxury of having a nanny *to* let her down.

'So, big Sis, I had a brainwave,' she went on. 'I thought of you. You're not doing anything, are you? You'd only need to have her till the Saturday, and then Tom could drive down and pick her up from you.'

Which would be a novelty. Ffion's ex-husband and I hadn't seen each other for about seven years, which was fine by me, and by him too, I didn't doubt. With all that had happened he was my least favourite person, and though I knew from Ffion that he'd remained a good dad, that didn't alter my opinion. The last time we'd met there'd been such a chill in the air I thought ice might start forming on my nose.

'Oh, I'd love to have Emily come and stay,' I said.

'She's off to stay at his parents' caravan for the week after that,' Ffion went on, clearly not hearing. 'And you *were* only saying the other day how long it had been since you last spent any time with Em.'

This was true. There were almost two weeks left of the summer holidays, and though I still had enough lesson planning to do to make me feel term should be postponed till October, it would be nice to leave it for a few days to spend them with my niece.

'Fine,' I said again. 'But you'll have to sort something else out for Tigger. Lovely though he is, I've got Ben at home from college.'

My son, Ben, had asthma. Not that badly, but my sister's big hairy dog wasn't exactly the ideal house-mate for him.

'Ah,' she said. 'I'd forgotten about that. I suppose I could – I know! Why don't you come here? To Cardiff? You're always saying how much you like my flat. And it'll be a nice break for you. You must be due a rest from running around after Ben and his mates.'

This was true, too. I loved having Ben around, but there were only so many times a day you could rant on about music being too loud and piles of washing-up being too high. It would also give me a chance to catch up with an old friend I hadn't seen for a while.

So I'd come to Cardiff, and here I was now, in an unfamiliar bedroom, with the throngs of people outside, the traffic, and the sticky city heat. But she was right. It did feel like a holiday.

I listened again. The buzzing had stopped, but now another noise had started up somewhere else. I pushed off the sheet, slipped on Ffion's old towelling dressing gown, then padded across the bedroom and into the hall. The phone there was silent, and there was no sound from Emily's room. The light from the hallway spilled through the open door and across her frame sprawled under the duvet. I walked across the hall, the wooden floor warm beneath my feet. The sound grew louder as I approached the study, louder still as I pushed open the door.

It was a living room really, with French doors that opened onto a little balcony. But Ffion had styled it in typical Ffion fashion.

High tech and sparse, with a beech desk and severe looking cupboards, this was the place where she worked much of the time. Her life was – always had been – very different from my own and I felt a little unsure about all the hardware and wires. Anxious that if I touched the wrong button, disaster would strike.

The fax machine at the side of the desk was now still, though it had been belching rolls of paper on and off since I'd arrived two days ago. Beside it, a green light winking on the computer reminded me it never slept. Another, a red one, had just clicked on to join it. Her work phone. Of course. Abruptly, the ringing stopped and the room was suddenly full of Ffion's voice. *'Hi. I can't get to the phone right now...'*. The greeting burbled on for some seconds, then a beep sounded.

'Ffion?' a voice said. 'God, it *is* you, isn't it? You sound...well, just the same. No different at all. Look, don't faint, but...well, it's Jack...'

The voice was male, rich like dark chocolate, it now paused for a second, as if unsure what to say next. I paused too, feeling a little like I was eavesdropping. It was just after midnight. So late to be calling. But then it could be one of her foreign authors. Ffion worked as a publicist for a big firm of publishers. It was her job to see their authors got noticed. She had always been good at getting herself noticed so it was no surprise she was so good at her job. That was how she'd first met Scott, her fiancé, a chef with two bestselling books already published. But this was probably nothing important. She'd told me not to worry about faxes and messages. She'd deal with them when she got back. I could let the man carry on and go back to bed.

I turned to leave him to it, but it was the silence, which continued for four or five more seconds, that made me pause to hear more. It was as if he really didn't know what to say.

'It's *me*, Ffion. *Jack*,' he repeated. 'I don't know if...well...' Another pause. A breath taken and exhaled. 'Oh, Ffion, I can hardly believe it. I can hardly believe I've...' Another breath. Another pause. 'Look, I'd just really like to speak to you. I *need* to speak to you, Ffion. Would you ring me? Please?'

He began reciting a number, but his pauses had been so long that the machine cut him off before he could finish it.

I stood still for several seconds, conscious that there was something about the message that was causing me disquiet. It wasn't anything I could put my finger on – just a nagging sense that this *was* something important. I'd never heard the name and I didn't know the voice, but this was clearly someone who knew Ffion well. No surnames. No sense of this being business. He knew she'd know exactly who he was. And he sounded intimate. Like someone who knew her very well, in fact.

I picked the receiver up and dialled 1471. *We do not have the number to return the call*, the voice told me. Perhaps he was ex-directory. I put the phone down again, pulling the dressing gown tighter around me, conscious of a draught and the click-clack of Tigger's feet on the beech flooring, as he came in to find out what was going on. If it was important, he'd call again, I reasoned, as I took the dog back into the kitchen. But still I dithered. It would now be early evening in New York. Perhaps I should give Ffion a quick ring anyway, just in case it *was* someone she'd been waiting to hear from. Yes, I'd go back and do that.

But she wasn't in her hotel room. Probably out at some party or other. She was on tour with an author, and these tours, I knew, were as much about fun as they were about meetings. I left a message. Just telling her there was nothing to worry about with Emily, but that there'd been a message on her work phone from someone called Jack.

I lay awake for some time after I got back into bed. I was sure she'd never mentioned a Jack to me before. Yet I also felt sure my gut response to his message was right. There was something about his words and manner that set off alarms in my head. 'Oh, Ffion...' he'd said. The words kept replaying. I'd been through all sorts of dramas with Ffion over the years. I hoped this wasn't about to become another one.

Hoping wasn't going to make any difference, of course. But I didn't know that, as I drifted back off to sleep.

CHAPTER TWO

'THOSE ARE *SO* NOT cool', moaned Emily as we stood at the till in the shoe shop the following morning and she frowned at the cream satin shoes in my hand.

'You will look like a princess,' I told her. I put them back in the box. Emily, just eleven and on the edge of scowling adolescence, viewed her mother's forthcoming wedding with a mixture of little-girl excitement and pre-teenage angst. Today was clearly one of the 'angst' days, but as bridesmaids didn't generally attend weddings in trainers, there wasn't much I could do about it.

I paid the shoe shop assistant for them and mentally ticked them off the list. Ffion never did miss a chance to delegate. I'd long since stopped trying to make her see that just because teachers weren't in school over the summer it didn't mean they weren't working. Besides, I thought now as my niece grinned up at me, there would be plenty of evenings for my school work, and far fewer chances to be spending time with her.

We headed back up St Mary Street and along to the department store, where Emily expressed similar dismay over the *so* sad little drawstring bag and headdress Ffion had chosen. But she brightened at the prospect of pizza for lunch.

'Shall we go now?' she asked eagerly.

I looked at my watch though I didn't really need to. 'It's not even eleven!'

'But I'm starving!' she said firmly. 'Anyway, we mustn't be late,' she reminded me. 'Hannah's mum is coming to collect me at three, remember, and I still have to get my jeans for the weekend.'

Another thing on the list. Emily couldn't possibly go to Gran and Grampy's caravan without the latest fashion must-haves. I smiled and reassured her I hadn't forgotten, and we headed off for our lunch.

The restaurant was half empty, and I chose a table by the sunny window while Emily trotted off to the Ladies. I was just sitting down when my mobile rang from my bag.

It was Ffion.

'Good grief,' I said. 'What time can it be there?'

'Around six,' she said. 'I just picked up your message.'

10

'Oh, sorry about that. But you know what it's like. I was worried it was something urgent, and –'

'So tell me.'

'There's not much to tell –'

'Tell it anyway. Exactly what he said.'

I shrugged off my jacket one-handed. When I'd woken that morning I'd felt there really wasn't that much to tell. What had seemed so haunting in the small hours seemed even less so after a dose of morning shopping. Probably it *was* just work, I'd decided. Or some old flame of no account. Ffion's voice, however, seemed to be telling me otherwise.

'Nothing very much,' I replied. 'Just that his name was Jack, and something about whether it was really you, and that he –'

'You're *sure* he said Jack?' she interrupted.

'Yes. Definitely. And that he – well, something along the lines of how he needed to speak to you – he mumbled a bit. He –'

'Did he leave a number?'

'Yes, but the machine cut him off before he could finish. I'm sure he'll –'

'Anything else? Did he say *anything* else?' Her voice was becoming agitated.

'No. Not really. Ffion, who is he? Is it something bad?'

11

She didn't answer straight away and I was about to prompt her when she spoke again.

'Jack,' she whispered. But it wasn't a question.

'Ffion, what is it?' I asked. *Don't faint*, he'd told her. 'You sound like you've just seen a ghost.'

Several seconds passed before she spoke again, her voice smaller still.

'Megan, I think I just have.'

But she refused to say more, and though there were all sorts of questions I wanted to ask her, Emily had returned. She plonked herself down beside me, wanting to know who was on the phone.

'Em's here,' I said to Ffion. 'Do you want a word with her?'

'Yes, please,' she said, still sounding odd. 'And Megan, look. It's nothing, OK?' Her voice was suddenly brisk again. 'Forget it.'

I handed Emily the phone and picked up my menu, reflecting that if this was about nothing, it was a type of nothing I'd never come across before.

CHAPTER THREE

BIG DOGS IN SMALL flats are not an easy mixture. Ffion had had Tigger for four years now, during which time he'd grown from a lively pup to an equally lively adult dog. He needed two good walks every day, if he was not to chew up everything that would fit between his jaws. Not the most sensible choice of pet. But Ffion had never counted 'sensible' among her list of virtues, and I knew Tigger made her feel more secure. Besides, she'd always said, with the hours she worked it was the only certain way to make sure she got any exercise.

I got plenty of that marching up and down the corridors of the sprawling high school I worked in. Walking dogs, therefore, was not on my own list of pastimes, but I was beginning to enjoy my strolls through town and down to the Bay. I watched the rest of the world go about its business, all of which, from my sleepy rural perspective, seemed to happen at double speed and to everyone at once. But there was a quiet little park not far from where Ffion lived, and once Emily had been dispatched with her friend for the afternoon, I put Tigger's lead on him and headed off there to think.

Not that there was much to think about. Just the name of a stranger, and my sister's response to his call. This had made it clear that not only had he meant something to her, but that he still *did* mean something, and I wanted to know what.

I skirted the flower garden and found a bench to sit down on, unclipping the lead from the collar so Tigger could have a run around. I knew it wasn't really any of my business, but as so much of Ffion's troubled life *had* been my business, it was difficult to break the habit.

We'd always been close, even though there were five years between us. As our parents were both in the forces and travelled so much, we spent a lot of time being the new girls in class, so we supported each other more than most. Our mother had died when we were still in our teens, and our father now lived, as he'd always hoped to, in the wilds of North Wales. We both got up to see him just a few times a year. These days, we didn't see much more of each other. But the bond was still there, especially when we were in trouble, and Ffion, who'd married young and, as it turned out, unwisely, had had more than her fair share of that.

But that was in the past, and she was happy now with Scott. It was a relief not to have to worry about her any more.

Except I did. Scott had called shortly after I'd returned from shopping. He wanted to know, as was his caring way, whether Emily and I wanted to come round for supper – he was having a few mates round for a barbecue. I'd explained about Emily going round to her friend's house, and we'd left things open, depending on when she got back. It was his call that had prompted me to go back into the study and listen to the message on the answer phone again. This time, I wrote down what I had of the number. Now, sitting in the park while Tigger checked out the wildlife, I brooded about what, if anything, to do.

I was just heading round the last corner before home when my mobile rang. It was Ffion again.

She was between a meeting and a book-signing, she said, and in the street somewhere, by the sound of it. I could barely make her out above the white noise in my ear.

'I can't stop,' she said. 'I'm using someone else's cell phone. But I thought I'd call.' Her breath was coming in gasps, so she must be walking. 'To see if Jack had called again.'

I paused by the hedge on the corner of the street. Not 'that man'. Jack.

'No,' I said. 'Not to my knowledge. But, look, Ffion, who *is* he? Is there some sort of problem?'

I could hear a blast on a horn in the background.

'No,' she said quickly. 'No problem. It's just that I need to speak to him, that's all. Look, if he calls again, would you speak to him and get his number? Or give him my number here? Yes. That's best. Or –'

'Or *what*? Ffion, I know this isn't any of my business, but you sound so stressed. Are you *sure* everything is OK?'

She laughed. But without any humour.

'OK as it can ever be, I guess,' she said. Then, 'No, *really*, Megan. Everything's fine.'

'Scott called earlier, by the way,' I added.

'I know. He just called me too.' Despite the din of street noise behind her, I could hear something almost sorrowful in her voice.

'Megan, Hi! It's so good to see you!'

By Friday lunchtime I was glad to have something else to do besides fretting. Debbie was one of my oldest friends, and was only too happy to travel down and 'do lunch' with me, as she put it. This suited Emily just fine, as she'd arranged to go swimming with a friend, so I had three hours all to myself. Debbie and I went back a long way – we'd done our teacher training together, and had worked at the same school until my ex-husband Owen and I had moved down to west Wales. I still wondered now about the wisdom of the move. I hadn't known, when we'd left all our friends, that our marriage wasn't going to last forever. I'd made new friends – good ones – but it was lovely to see her.

We found a table for two on the outer edge of one of the vast café restaurants in Cardiff Bay. Another hot day meant it was busy with pink-faced office workers and hungry tourists.

'So,' she said, as the waiter came to take our orders for drinks. 'How's things? Enjoying your holiday?'

'I don't know about holiday,' I told her. 'But it's great to see Em, and have a break from work, of course.'

She nodded. 'Tell me about it! When are you going back?'

'Sunday. Tom's coming to collect Emily on Saturday to take her to his parents. She's spending the week with them. But I'm staying till Ffion gets back. One last night of dog-sitting to do.'

She narrowed her eyes.

'Tom? There's a name I won't forget in a hurry. He's still around then?'

'Never hasn't been,' I said, shaking my head.

She picked up her menu. 'Now you do surprise me. I thought he'd have been long gone. I had him down for Christmas and birthday cards only, to be honest. So,' she said, opening the menu, 'seems I stand corrected. What's he up to these days? Married again?'

I thought back to the affair that had finally, explosively, ended Tom and Ffion's marriage. He'd split up with the girl he'd been seeing soon after. I didn't know what he'd been up to since. I didn't much care. Ffion and I never talked about it.

'I wouldn't know,' I said. 'But I expect so. I'm only glad to see Ffion so happy at last.'

If that's what she was. Who was Jack? What was happening? As I opened my menu, I couldn't help but fret. I didn't want to see her hurt again.

CHAPTER FOUR

SEEING TOM AGAIN WASN'T something that should have caused me a moment's worry. He was simply my sister's ex-husband, and however many rows we'd had in the bad days, it was water under the bridge by now. Even so, when Emily called to tell me his car had just pulled up outside, I couldn't control the little knot of discomfort that suddenly tightened in my tummy.

We'd known each other a long time, of course. Ffion had met him when she was just seventeen, and married him not long after. And just like any young couple, they'd been very happy at first. But it didn't last. Ffion had always been a person of extremes, up one minute and down the next. By the time they'd been married a couple of years she seemed to be down all the time. And when she found she was expecting Emily she cried for two days, as if her whole world had fallen apart. We all thought she'd rally once the baby was born, but then she'd become ill with post-natal depression. At first, I took on much of the baby minding, but we'd all assumed Tom would see Ffion through it.

But as things went from bad to worse, he became more remote and unsupportive. Gradually it became clear that the cause of Ffion's depression wasn't Emily at all, but *him*. Even so, I'd hoped they might see their way through it, but then he nearly destroyed her, by betraying her in the time-honoured way. It was no wonder I didn't think much of him. For Ffion it had been a very, very long haul back.

But that was history. I must try to be polite to him. I finished pulling my hair into a ponytail and went to open the front door.

He'd changed very little since the last time I'd seen him. He had the same handsome face, the same flop of blond fringe, the same piercing blue eyes, the same lopsided grin. Only the lines that creased his face as he smiled marked the passing of the years.

'Hello!' he said cheerfully, as the sunlight puddled on the floor at my feet. 'Are the troops ready for the off?'

I ushered him in, feeling a little out of place in Ffion's hallway all of a sudden, and disarmed by how friendly he was.

'Almost,' I said, returning his smile politely.

'We're just fine-tuning on the accessories front. I hope you brought a trailer.' I pointed to the pile of Emily's stuff on the hall floor. Sleeping bag, two pillows, case and back pack, portable CD player, teddy, rollerblades. He frowned.

'Just the *one* trailer?' He stooped to pick the case up and grinned up at me. 'You're looking well, Megan. How's things?'

I wondered if he knew about my own divorce. Probably, I reasoned. He and Ffion got along well enough these days. She would have told him.

'Fine,' I said, picking up the pillows and sleeping bag. 'Still teaching. Still trying to flog Shakespeare to the masses. Pleased to have a bit of time off, to be honest. How about you?'

I followed him down the short flight of steps to the road. His car was parked a few doors away, the boot already open.

'Much the same,' he said, plonking the case in and holding his arms out for the pile in mine. 'I'm still with Peterson's.'

Peterson's, the firm of engineers he'd been with most of his working life. And judging by the car, he was fairly high up the ladder now. He may have been a rat to my sister but he'd always been a hard worker.

21

'Building anything interesting right now?'

'A hotel in Swansea, as it happens.'

'That's nice.'

We walked back to the flat to collect the rest of Emily's stuff, our polite chitchat grinding to a halt. But, thankfully, Emily herself was on the doorstep.

'Right then,' he said, pulling his keys from his pocket. 'Tell Ffion I'll drop her back about this time next week.' I nodded. 'She's got Dad's mobile number?' I nodded again. Emily gave me a hug and headed off down to the car.

'Well,' he said. 'Nice to see you again.' Then he grinned at me. 'Really. I mean it!' He turned and was off down the road.

As I stepped back inside and closed the front door, I imagined that would probably be the last I'd see of Tom for another few years. The sunlight was fading now, but it was still warm, and after I'd walked the dog the prospect of a salad and a couple of glasses of wine on the balcony felt good. I really must stop fretting about my sister. Ffion had called to speak to Emily just before she went, but our own chat had been brief. No, he hadn't called again, I'd told her, and this time she'd sounded less anxious about it. Probably I'd been worrying over nothing. Force of habit, I guessed sadly, as I took Tigger's lead from its hook.

Half an hour and a sprint round the block later, I was all set to take my picnic out on to the balcony. I was just looking for a corkscrew when the phone rang in the hall. I put the bottle down and went out to answer it. It was Tom.

'Houston?' he said, all pretend-American. 'We have a problem.'

I laughed, despite myself. I hadn't heard that expression for years. I expected it, of course, given the surname I'd married into, and with Tom it had stuck. He used to say it to me all the time.

Before we became enemies, that is. 'Ho ho,' I answered. 'Which is?'

'She's forgotten to pack her Madonna CD. The end of the world, of course. Could I pop back and pick it up later? It's in the CD player in her room, she said. She's got the case.'

'No problem,' I said. 'I'm not going anywhere. Come round when you're ready, I'll get it out for you now.'

It was while I was doing so that I heard a familiar voice once again. Had Tom not called,

23

and I'd been outside, I probably wouldn't have heard it. I moved quickly from the living room to the study, reaching the phone just as Ffion's greeting message clicked off. The machine beeped once.

'Ffion?' It was him. 'It's Jack again –' I didn't leave him to finish his sentence this time, but picked up the receiver and put it to my ear.

'It's not Ffion,' I said. 'She's away. This is Megan, her sister. Can I take a message?'

But before I'd got the last of the words out, he'd hung up the phone.

'The things you do,' said Tom regretfully, waiting while I fetched the CD. Since the second call, I'd become anxious again. It was now gone ten and I could think of little else. Who was this man? I'd tried calling Ffion, but she was out again. In a meeting at the conference centre, the girl on the hotel switchboard told me. And by the time she came back it would be the small hours here, so I decided I wouldn't leave a message. She'd be off to the airport soon, anyway. Her flight back was due in at Heathrow late morning. Perhaps then I'd get some answers.

I got the CD from the kitchen where I'd left

it, and popped it into the case Tom was holding out. He flipped it shut with a snap.

'Never let it be said that I don't suffer for my daughter,' he said, laughing. 'The traffic is appalling. Where does it all come from?'

He looked tired. 'Look, do you want to stop for a coffee or something?' I asked him.

He hovered, unsure, then looked at his watch. 'Thanks, but I'd really better get back. I'm supposed to be on site first thing in the morning.' He made a face. 'There ought to be a law against it. You off in the morning?'

I shook my head. 'Afternoon. I'm going to stay till Ffion gets back.'

In saying so, it occurred to me that perhaps Tom could shed some light on who her mystery man was. Unlikely, but it couldn't hurt to ask, could it?

'Tom,' I said, as he turned to open the front door. 'Ffion's never mentioned someone called Jack to you, has she? It's just that a man called Jack has been trying to get in touch with her, and –'

He spun around. 'Jack?'

'Some guy she knows. I don't know who he is, but he's rung a couple of times, and seems very anxious to speak to her, and he sounds, I don't know, like...'

'*Jack*?' he asked again.

I nodded. 'It's silly, but there's something about his voice that –' I stopped, abruptly.

Despite the sodium glare from the streetlight outside, every drop of colour had drained from Tom's face.

CHAPTER FIVE

A LONG MOMENT PASSED while Tom stood there, just staring.

'What is it?' I said, suddenly full of anxiety. 'Do you know who this Jack is?'

He turned and looked out towards the street, then back at me again, his eyes not quite focussing, as if he was staring into space. Then he drew his hand across his hair, and shook his head.

'No, no,' he replied, turning the CD case over and over in his hands. 'I don't think so. No. Can't help you, I'm afraid.'

He was lying. I was sure of it. But *why*?

'Are you *sure*?' I persisted. But by now he was down the steps and on to the path. He waggled the CD case at me. 'Better get off. And, er, well…goodnight.'

I nearly ran down the path after him, to demand answers, but everything about his manner told me there would be no point. Whatever it was he knew about this Jack person, he plainly wasn't about to tell me.

It was something*neither* of them would tell me, which perhaps was telling me that it really was nothing to do with me. So maybe I should just go to bed and put the whole thing out of my mind. If there was something going on, and Ffion *was* in some sort of trouble, then I didn't doubt she'd tell me in her own good time.

I shut the door and flicked off the hall light. But what sort of trouble could she be in? Was this something to do with Scott? Was this Jack someone who had some sort of hold over her? When my mind started wandering to criminals and blackmail and all sorts, I knew it was time to rein myself in. This was just someone who'd phoned, called Jack, who knew Ffion. It really was none of my business. It would only become so if Ffion wanted it to be. Perhaps she'd lay my fears to rest tomorrow.

I'd checked the note on Ffion's message board and found out that her flight was due in at midday. It was with some shock therefore that I answered the phone at eleven thirty on Sunday morning to hear Ffion's voice.

'Oh!' I said, 'You're at Heathrow already are you? Good flight?'

'Fine,' she said. She sounded very brisk. 'We had a tail wind. Listen. Could you do me a really big favour, Megan? There's a suit at the cleaners I need. I've got to go off to a Roadshow first thing Monday and I forgot to pick it up before I left last week.' She'd told me about Roadshows before. The publishers took their top authors out to meet booksellers, and presented their latest bestsellers to them. This one was to be at a hotel in Manchester, apparently. 'You couldn't be an angel,' she went on, 'and collect it for me, could you? By the time I get home they'll be closed.'

'Are they open on a Sunday?'

'Oh, yes,' she said. 'The ticket's pinned to the board in the kitchen. It's pink. You can't miss it. Lewis's. They're not far. Just up towards –'

'Hang on,' I said. 'I'd better grab a pen.'

She gave me a complicated list of directions. I could take my car, she said, but as it could be difficult to park, I'd probably be better off walking. She knew it was a dreadful cheek to ask, but I didn't mind, did I?

I said I didn't. It was a nice enough morning, and I had been planning to pop out and get something in for lunch anyway. It was reassuring to hear her sounding so bright and breezy. Perhaps the Jack problem had solved itself. Perhaps he'd got hold of her in New York.

Perhaps I should break the habit of a lifetime and stop worrying about my little sister, full stop.

I found the ticket, put the directions in my pocket, fed Tigger, and set off.

By the time I had collected the suit – a rather stylish-looking red one – the earlier sunshine had been obscured by a blanket of cloud, and a thin drizzle had started. It would make the journey home less enjoyable than it might have been, but at least the humidity of the previous few days had lessened.

Rounding the corner of Ffion's road, I decided I'd give my son a quick call, to fill him in on my plans.

'There you are, Mum!' he said. 'I've been trying you for ages!'

'Oh, dear,' I said. 'Is there a panic of some sort? Have you burned the house down?'

'*No*, mother. Well, only the garage.' He laughed. 'Joke. I just wanted to make sure you hadn't forgotten I'm off to David's this afternoon.'

Something about a surfing trip rang a distant bell. I had forgotten.

'You could have called me at Auntie Ffion's,' I reminded him.

'Might have been able to, if only I could read the writing in your address book.' Which was fair comment. My address book, which I'd had since the day of my wedding, had become somewhat chaotic over the years. 'You shouldn't keep switching your phone off,' he told me.

'I had to. Emily and I went to the pictures on Friday night.'

'I told you, Mum. You don't need to do that. Just put it on silent and vibrate. Then you'll be able to feel it instead.'

'Yes, yes,' I said. 'Anyway, I won't be back till teatime so just make sure you don't leave the place like a bomb site, OK?'

Then I stood and scrolled down the menu on my phone till I found 'silent'. I clicked. The wonders, I thought, of modern technology. I really must make friends with it sometime.

It was a little after one by the time I got back, but there was no sign of Ffion. I wasn't sure how long it would take her to drive from the airport. Judging by what Tom had said about the traffic the previous evening, it could be some time. I went into the bedroom. I might as well get my things together. I'd pulled my suitcase up on to the bed and had just started going through the wardrobe, when I heard a strange noise somewhere close by. A buzzing sound, which seemed to be coming from my handbag. I picked it up, and realisation dawned. Inside, my mobile phone was now lit up *and* vibrating.

It was Ben again, to tell me he was just leaving. I wished him a good trip and slung the phone back down on the bed, and then something else occurred to me. That noise had been exactly the sound that had woken me on Wednesday night. A mobile phone vibrating. *Ffion's* mobile, which she'd left behind, because it didn't work in the States. It had been sitting in the corner of her kitchen worktop, plugged into its charger the whole time.

The name Jack once again popped into my mind. He must have rung the mobile first. Still telling myself off for once again following my nose instead of my common sense, I decided to take a look. Perhaps he'd left a message and his number there as well. I went into the kitchen. The charger was still plugged into the socket, but the mobile had disappeared.

How odd. How could that be? I looked all around but the phone was nowhere to be seen. It had still been there when I'd left to go out, so how could it not be now? And then something else occurred to me. Something else I was sure I'd seen or felt or heard. But what? I went back into the bedroom and nothing seemed any different, nor in the living room. But as soon as I went in the study there was something I did notice. The red light that had been winking ever since that first message from Jack was now glowing steadily. The messages had been erased.

So someone had been in the flat while I'd been out. But who? Had *he*? I tutted at myself. No. That was plainly stupid. The place was locked up. Tigger would have barked. It had to be someone who – that was it! Ffion! *Ffion* had been here. The thing that had been nagging at me was the scent of her perfume as I'd walked in the door. She'd been here and gone out again. But how could she have got back from Heathrow airport so quickly? Another thought, less comforting, hit me. That maybe she'd sent me off to get her suit from the cleaners because she didn't want me to be here when she arrived. The erased messages seemed to prove it. This was something to do with Jack.

The sensible thing to do was to call her on her mobile. But, as I suspected even before I'd found her number in my own phone, her phone didn't answer. It simply rang and rang. So there was nothing to do but carry on with my packing and await her return.

Four o'clock came and went. I was angry now. She hadn't thought to let me know what she was up to – and at the very least she should consider that I had work to get done and couldn't sit with her dog forever. I was just bumping my suitcase down the steps to my car when hers pulled up outside.

She smiled as she saw me, but there was something else in her expression. Something I recognised from when we'd both been teenagers and she'd 'borrowed' one of my tops for the night.

She got out of the car, colouring a little.

'I'm *so* sorry, Sis,' she said. 'You must have been wondering where on earth I've been. There was an accident on the M4. I've been stuck for hours.'

I stood my case by the front garden gate and looked squarely at her.

'No, there wasn't,' I said. 'You've been back here.'

She blinked at me. 'No, I –'

'Look, Ffion, if you don't want to tell me what it's all about, fine, but at least stop all this cloak-and-dagger stuff.'

She held my gaze for a second, then dropped her eyes and seemed to crumple inside her clothes. She shut the car door and headed up the pavement towards me, looking as vulnerable, suddenly, as she'd done all those years ago.

'Megan, look, I'm sorry, OK. You're absolutely right.'

'And?'

She glanced up at the clouds. 'Let's get inside.'

CHAPTER SIX

I DIDN'T KNOW WHAT I expected my sister to tell me, but the look on her face was already telling me a great deal. Yes, she had been back, yes she had got hold of Jack, but, no, she couldn't tell me any more than that.

'But *why* can't you?' I insisted. 'What's it all about?' She looked, by this time, close to tears. 'Is it something to do with Scott?'

She perched herself on one of the two stools in the kitchen. A single tear tracked down her cheek.

'It's nothing to do with Scott,' she said, brushing it away and sniffing. Her hands were shaking. 'Well, it is, in a way, but, look, Megan, you must understand that it's really nothing to do with *you*.' She said this gently, as if to reassure me that she didn't mean for me to be offended. I wasn't sure where to go next. Years ago I had sat with her in much the same way, Ffion dulled by anti-depressants and resolutely not speaking, me wondering how on earth to get her to talk to me. It suddenly felt like only yesterday.

'So you're telling me everything's all right, then. Is that it?'

'As far as you're concerned, yes. I'm sorry, but this isn't something I can share with you, Megan. I really don't want you to become involved, OK? There's nothing you can do about it. There's nothing *to* do. Jack was – is – someone I once knew, that's all. And I've heard from him. And I've been in touch with him. And it's...well...' She seemed to be choosing her words very carefully. 'It's brought back some painful memories, that's all.'

I took her hand and squeezed it.

'I just wish you'd tell me *what*. I hate going off and leaving you in such a state.'

She composed herself and stood up. 'Megan, you can't sort this one out for me. I know you worry, but I'm an adult and I will sort it out myself. I'll be fine.'

I had to be satisfied with that. Ffion was my sister, after all, not my daughter, however much it might have felt that way after our mum died. She'd made it perfectly plain that I wasn't to be involved, and that things were going to stay that way. Nevertheless, it was with an entirely put-on smile on my face that I left the flat an hour later. Old habits, I thought as I drove, died hard.

Being physically removed from Ffion's problems was always helpful. Back in west Wales I would have heaps of work to do – a meeting to attend in the morning, and all that new term's planning that I should have been doing all week. She wasn't my responsibility. I would just have to put it out of my mind.

At home, I unpacked and decided to get myself organised. I was hungry, for one thing. Though Ben had left the place pretty tidy (only a smallish hillock in the wash basket) there was nothing but a jar of pickled chillies in the fridge. I would pop to the shops, then get down to some work. When I'd called Ffion to let her know I'd got home safely, she sounded much more like her usual breezy self. Quite jolly, in fact, so much so that I was almost convinced it was genuine. I began to wonder, yet again, if I hadn't blown things up out of all proportion.

On Monday morning, however, when I was sorting through my handbag, I realised I'd come home with all her house keys. In the tense half hour following her return, I'd completely forgotten to give them back. She had another front door key, of course, but the keyring in my hand held all the rest. She'd no doubt realise I had them, but it would be a good excuse to get in touch. I tried her mobile, but it didn't answer, and then I remembered she'd said she was driving to Manchester, so before I set off for my meeting at school, I rang her office instead.

I dialled the main switchboard, and was soon connected to Marie in the publicity office. I'd spoken to Marie before and she greeted me warmly, chattily asking about my week at Ffion's, before asking what she could help me with.

'I was wondering if you had a number for Ffion at the hotel.' I explained about the keys.

'Hotel?'

'In Manchester,' I said. 'Only I didn't want her to worry –'

'Manchester? She's not in Manchester. Well, not as far as I know. She's had to take a couple of days leave. She's not back in till...let me see...' I could hear the sound of pages being flicked. 'Thursday. Yes. She'll be back on Thursday. We've got a cover meeting for Scott's next title, as it happens, and I know she wanted to be back for that. But if she calls in, I'll certainly let her know.'

'Oh,' I said, my worries returning like a swarm of angry wasps. 'I didn't realise. She never said.'

'Well, she only just let *me* know. She called me at home last night...' A pause. 'You don't think something's wrong, do you?'

I wondered if I should confide in Marie. No, I decided. No sense in making a drama out of a crisis. Or a crisis out of drama, even. Ffion had always been good at dramas.

'Oh, I'm sure there isn't,' I said, trying to believe it myself. 'I'm sure I'll catch up with her on her mobile later. But if you do speak to her, let her know I called, won't you?'

I was due in school in less than thirty minutes, but after I put the phone down, I couldn't seem to galvanise myself to get out of the door. What on earth was going on? Where had she gone? My sister had been many things over the years. Depressed, unhappy, difficult. But a liar? Never. Yet she'd now lied to me twice in as many days.

CHAPTER SEVEN

I TRIED THE FLAT. No answer. I tried Ffion's mobile again. Ditto. Vaguely, I wondered what was happening with the dog. What on earth was she *doing*? Should I ring Scott? No. That might be the last thing she wanted. I picked up my school bag and tried hard to keep calm. Keep your nose out, I told myself. Don't worry. Don't get involved. On the other hand...I wondered. Yes. On the other hand, I could ring Tom.

It didn't take more than a couple of minutes to get Petersons' number from directory enquiries, and thirty seconds later I was calling his office, and scribbling his mobile number on the pad by the phone.

He was on site. The steady thump of heavy machines almost drowned out his voice.

'Hang on,' he said, once I'd told him who it was. 'I'll find somewhere quieter.'

The din began to ease up.

'Hi, Megan,' he said. He didn't sound remotely surprised to be hearing from me. Just resigned. Which was telling. He sighed. 'What is it?'

I told him about Ffion's sudden disappearance.

'I'm sorry to be bothering you with this,' I finished. 'Only I'm...well...' Well what? She could just be out shopping, couldn't she? No. I knew my sister too well. And Tom. I took a breath. 'Only I'm not sure you were being completely honest with me on Saturday evening, Tom. You *do* know something about this Jack guy, don't you?'

The silence that greeted this statement told me I'd been right. He *had* lied. Nothing new there, then.

'Yes,' he said finally. 'Well, yes and no. I do know of *a* Jack.' He paused again.

'And?'

'But he's dead, Megan. He's been dead twelve years.' I heard this statement along with a clamour of bell-ringing. A *ghost*. She said she'd seen a ghost. What on earth was all this about? 'So it can't be him, can it?' he finished.

I sat down by the phone, my mind spinning. Someone she used to know. Someone who brought back painful memories. But *what* memories? 'I think perhaps it can,' I said. 'Are you absolutely *sure* he's dead? Who *was* he?'

'Megan, look,' he answered. 'I can't talk to you right now. Someone's waiting for me. Can I call you back?'

'Tom, can't you just tell me? How do you know this Jack? Who is he? Who *was* he?'

He sighed again.

'Megan, give me your number, and I'll get back to you once I'm finished here.'

There was no point trying to hassle him. I gave him my number.

'But I'm off out now. School meeting. We'll finish around two. Can we talk then?'

'OK,' he said. 'I'll call you at two.'

The meeting seemed to go on forever. The weather was gearing itself up for a storm and the walls of the staff room pressed in on all sides. But we finished a little after one, and, reluctantly saying no to a trip to the local pub for some lunch, I headed straight home to take Tom's call.

I got there a little after one-thirty. I let myself in and threw open half a dozen downstairs windows. I'd tried Ffion's mobile again without success, and when the phone rang I thought it might be her. But it was her fiancé, Scott.

'Sorry to trouble you,' he said. 'But Ffion isn't with you, is she?'

'No,' I answered. 'I've been trying to get hold of her myself, as it happens.'

'Hmm,' he said. 'It's just she just seemed a bit, I don't know, *odd* last night. And she's not in her office, and I can't reach her on her mobile. I was wondering if she'd said anything to you.'

I wasn't sure whether to tell him or not. I needed to speak to Tom.

'Probably off at a signing or something,' I said, trying to keep my voice light. 'Or out on a secret wedding dress mission, perhaps.'

'Hmm,' he said again. 'Oh, well. I dare say she'll turn up later. No problem.'

I fervently hoped he was right.

44

CHAPTER EIGHT

IT WAS WELL PAST two by the time Tom called back.

'So,' he said, without preamble. 'Have you tracked Ffion down?'

'No,' I replied. 'And her fiancé's just been on the phone. He hasn't seen anything of her either. Look, I know Ffion's problems are really nothing to do with you any more, but whatever you know about this guy, I'd really appreciate knowing too. I have a huge pile of paperwork to get through and I could really do without all this angst.'

'Just like old times, eh?'

'Quite.'

'OK.' He sounded apologetic. 'Look, I've racked my brains and I don't see any way it can be him. Like I said, the only Jack I knew died a long time ago in a car crash.'

'But who was he?'

His voice was short. 'A guy she was in love with.'

An old boyfriend. I had guessed as much. 'But how did *you* –'

45

'Houston, you are a *teensy* bit slow on the uptake. Because she was married to *me* at the time. You get the drift?'

I got the drift. 'You mean she was seeing this guy when –'

'Yes,' he said shortly.

I was stunned. *Ffion*? An *affair*? Ffion who'd sat and wept endlessly in my arms about her marriage? Ffion who'd been so hurt by Tom? Ffion, who'd spent at least a year of her life barely able to function, let alone go gadding around seeing other men?

'I can't believe it,' I said finally. 'When? For how long?'

'Two and a half, three years. I don't know exactly when it started, but I can tell you exactly when it finished.'

'When?'

'When he died, of course.'

I was thinking fast now. 'Or didn't. How did you find out?'

'Ffion told me, of course.'

Another lie? No. She must have believed it herself. Why else react as she did when Jack had called? 'Well, there can't be two of them, surely? And it all makes sense. It must be him. Tom, believe me, when I said his name, it was as if she'd been hit by a truck.'

46

He sounded thoughtful. 'And you think she's gone somewhere to meet him?'

'I don't know what to think. She said she'd been in touch with him when she came back on Sunday. But would something – someone – from so long ago *really* have such a dramatic effect?'

'This is Ffion we're talking about,' he said, echoing my own thoughts. 'You don't know the half of it, Megan. Really you don't.'

But I was beginning to. It all suddenly seemed to fit. Her depression, her illness, Tom's affair.

'I'm stunned,' I said. 'God, Tom. How did I manage not to *know* about this? I can't believe she never told me about him. And all the while I was thinking *you* were cheating on *her*.'

'It wasn't up to me to put you straight, Megan.'

'I'm sorry. I know that. But how come I never *sensed* it? Had any idea, even?'

'Why would you?' he said wryly. 'I didn't.'

I couldn't begin to imagine how much I'd got wrong. 'So he's alive, and now he's found her again – but why should she be so secretive about it? I mean, you've been divorced eight years. Unless...I mean, what about Scott?' I thought for a moment and answered my own question. 'I suppose she wants to see him – I mean, if you thought someone you cared about had been dead for years and they suddenly showed up, then you *would* want to see them, wouldn't you? And I suppose with Scott – well, she wouldn't want him to know, would she? Not if she hadn't told him.'

'Oh, believe me, she wouldn't have told Scott about Jack.'

'So she's probably gone off to meet him somewhere and hopefully that'll be that.' I was shocked, but relieved as well. If only she'd told me before. 'And she's right,' I said. 'It isn't any of my business. Whatever he *was* to her, well, twelve years is a very long time, and –'

'Megan,' he interrupted. 'It's not as simple as that. If this Jack is the one I'm talking about...' He paused for a long moment.

'*What?*' I said.

'He's Emily's father.'

CHAPTER NINE

I WAS AT A loss for words. Not so much because I couldn't *find* the words, but because there were so *many* of them, all fighting for space in my brain. I couldn't believe it, yet it must be true. Who would joke about something like that?

'I can't believe you just told me that,' I said to Tom.

'It's true, nevertheless,' he said. His voice had changed, had become flat and toneless. No wonder he'd looked so upset on Saturday when I'd asked him if he knew who Jack was.

'But how –' I began. 'I mean, have you *always* known? And what about Ffion? And what about Emily? Does *she* know?'

'No.' There was an edge to his voice now. 'She knows nothing about it, and she isn't about to. Megan, I...look. We need to talk. *I* need to talk. But I have to get back to work. Can I call you later? Or better still, can we meet up? Have you got anything on this evening?'

Anything I might have been doing would have seemed trivial in comparison. But it was

Monday evening, and I had nothing more pressing to attend to than a basket of ironing.

'Of course we need to talk,' I said. 'But you're in Cardiff and I'm out here. Do you want to meet somewhere halfway?'

'Where's here?' he asked. Of course. He'd no reason to know where I lived these days.

'It's a village just outside Pembroke,' I told him. I gave him the details. 'So I guess we could meet up somewhere near the motorway –'

'No, no,' he interrupted. 'I'll come to you. Shouldn't take me more than a couple of hours. I'll finish up here and drive straight down. Say be there around seven?'

'Don't you have to get home?'

'I'm sure the cat will cope,' he said grimly.

The afternoon, now hijacked, stretched before me, but there was no question of getting any more work done today. Emily not Tom's daughter? I still couldn't believe it. More incredible still was that during all the years Ffion had confided in me she never let slip even the tiniest hint about all this. What had she done? How did it all happen? Why was Tom bringing up another man's child?

But going over and over it was pointless. The answers I wanted would be coming with Tom, at seven.

He arrived at a quarter to. He'd called me for directions five minutes before. When he arrived, I was trying to revive the neglected tubs of flowers in the front garden. He slammed the door of the car and walked up the path, shoulders slightly drooped.

'A lost cause, I think,' he said, nodding towards the flowers.

I put down my watering can and led him inside.

'Forgot to remind my son to water them,' I said regretfully. 'Are you hungry?'

He shook his head as he took off his jacket and yanked at the knot of his tie. I pulled out a chair for him at the kitchen table, feeling all at once self-conscious. And guilty, as well, that I'd spent so many years angry with him. 'A drink, then?'

'Something cold, if you've got it,' he said, sitting down and ploughing both his hands through his hair. He'd been just twenty-one when Ffion first introduced us, a couple of years younger than me. And though his hair had been a foot longer back then, the action was instantly, unmistakeably the same Tom. I

51

went over to the fridge and pulled out a carton of juice. He watched me as I poured from it into two tumblers.

'I was sorry to hear about your divorce,' he said. I put his glass down in front of him.

I pulled out another chair and sat down opposite. 'So was I.'

'What happened? If you don't mind me asking.'

I smiled at him. 'Not at all. Nothing dramatic. I leave all the dramas to Ffion.'

I grinned as I said this, but his expression was sad. 'So what *did* happen?'

'We just grew apart, I guess. The usual story. But it feels like a long time ago now.' I was conscious of a questioning look on his face. 'It's *fine*. I'm OK. Happy, even.'

'Well, that's good.'

I smiled. 'It was the right thing to do.'

He took a long swallow from his glass and returned it to the table half empty.

'Ah,' he said. 'The right thing. Yes. Have you heard anything yet, by the way?'

'No. I tried her mobile again. And the flat, of course. But no. God knows where she is.' I waited, uncomfortable now about how to start the conversation that I'd been playing in my head all afternoon.

'Wherever *he* is, no doubt,' he said, picking up his glass again. He finished it, and looked grimly at me. 'So,' he said at last. 'Where do I start?'

'Wherever you like, Tom. It's your bombshell.'

'Well, there's plenty I don't know,' he said. 'When Ffion told me, Emily must have been eight or nine months old. That was the first I knew of it. Actually, that's not completely true. I'd suspected she was seeing someone else long before she fell pregnant with Em. Back when she was doing PR for that firm in Swansea. You remember? Doing that re-launch package for the hospital?' I nodded. They'd lived near Swansea then. That would have been about two years after they were married.

Tom continued, 'I didn't ever confront her about it. And – I don't know – I suppose I just hoped I was imagining it. Nothing much happened. Nothing concrete. I guess I just drew a line under it.' He linked his hands on the table. 'And once she was pregnant, I thought we were moving forward again. She seemed brighter. More positive. Less withdrawn.'

Which wasn't the way she'd seemed when she first told *me* about her pregnancy. Why would that be? There was so much I didn't understand.

'I knew nothing right through the pregnancy, of course, and long after the birth. I'm not even sure why she *did* tell me,' he went on. Then he frowned. 'She was still really ill at that time'.

I mentally back-tracked. Ffion's mental state had got much worse after the birth. She'd been admitted with severe post-natal depression and spent over two months in hospital. It had been a terrible time. 'She was still an outpatient then, wasn't she?'

He nodded. 'And still dosed up on drugs and seeing the psychologist. I remember the day, though. You know, I sometimes wonder if those counselling visits had something to do with it. She'd been having sessions every week, and I'd thought they seemed to be doing her good. She was getting her spark back a bit, you know?' I did know. It had been like a light coming back on after a long period in the dark.

I nodded. 'So what happened?'

'She was just sitting there when I got back from work one evening, and said "Tom, there's something important I have to tell you" and that was that. She told me. It was surreal. She said she'd been seeing this guy for a long time, that she'd been going to leave me but that he'd been killed in a car accident, and that Emily was not mine but his. And that she pretended Em *was* mine because she simply hadn't known what else to do.'

I felt a sudden rush of sympathy for him. It must have been so awful. I almost wanted to hug him. 'Just like that?'

'Just like that.' He gave me a wry grin. 'Only more so. It was as if she was doing an audition for drama school. Heaven only knows how long she'd been rehearsing her lines. Anyway, then she broke down and said she couldn't live the lie any longer. That she hoped I could forgive her and that we could still make things work.'

'And you did.'

His blue eyes bored into mine. 'Sounds so simple, doesn't it? But, oh, no. Not then I didn't. I didn't have the first clue what *to* do. My first thought – my gut instinct – was that there was no way on earth I could forgive her. Not because I was shocked by the affair – as I told you, things hadn't been brilliant – but because of Emily. Which meant my second thought was, how could I *not* forgive her? How could I let Emily go?'

55

'I can't imagine what it must have felt like. I mean, you –'

He spread his hands in front of me. 'I'd watched her being born. Taken care of her. *Loved* her. No matter how difficult I knew it would be, I was *not* going to lose my daughter.' He looked straight at me. 'And she *is* my daughter, Megan. It's my name on the birth certificate. And there is no way on earth that anything, or *anyone*, is going to change that.'

CHAPTER TEN

TOM SEEMED IN NO hurry to leave, so I cooked us pasta while he opened the bottle of wine I'd tucked away in the fridge the previous evening. It felt strange to be sharing a meal with the man I'd disliked so much for such a big chunk of my life. Who I'd been so horrible to, when he didn't deserve it.

'I owe you one hell of an apology,' I said, as we brought our plates to the table. All those rows. All the dreadful things I'd said to him. And meant.

He smiled and shook his head. 'No, you don't, Megan. You didn't know the truth, so I'm not surprised you hated me.'

'But Ffion. I mean, she let me think you'd treated her so badly. You must feel bitter about that, surely?'

He poured wine into our glasses. 'I felt unhappy that you didn't know the truth. That you thought so little of me. But bitter? No. Not that. This isn't about villains and victims, Megan. I knew perfectly well what I was taking on when I said I'd stay. I knew she didn't love me. And I'd be lying if I said I still felt anything for her by then. But I made the decision anyway. I guess I was –' he grinned as he raised his glass to me, '– an idealist, if you like. I thought we could make it work for Emily's sake. And a part of me – well, it sounds like a cliché, but it was true – a part of me felt I had a *duty* to stay. What would Ffion do? How would she cope on her own? She'd been sick for a very long time.'

'Not sick,' I said, feeling all at once furious with my sister in the face of Tom's refusal to blame her. 'She *wasn't* sick, Tom. She was grieving for Jack! And feeling guilty. As she had every reason to!'

He seemed to understand my anger.

'I know what you're saying,' he said, smiling. 'But you forget, I've had years to come to terms with things. Whatever the rights and wrongs, she did what she did because she thought it was the only thing *to* do. There's no point going over it again now.'

I stabbed at my pasta with my fork, feeling guilty myself. For seeing everything in black and white. For just accepting that it had all been Tom's fault, when it hadn't.

I returned his smile. 'You sound remarkably calm about it.'

'I am. *Now*. I wasn't always. I couldn't keep it up any more than she could.'

'Your affair —'

'Was nothing. But I'm a normal human being.' He gazed at me over the rim of his glass. 'And there's only so long you can go without some love and affection in your life. It was over before the ink was dry on the divorce papers.'

'And now?'

He put his wine down. 'And now nothing. There have been a couple of relationships, but, well, I have a daughter, for one thing, and...well, let's just say I'm not *quite* the idealist I once was. A little more wary of getting involved again, perhaps. Once bitten, twice shy...'

I nodded. 'That strikes a chord,' I said, feeling shy myself now under his gaze.

'So that makes two of us,' he said, picking his glass up again. 'Let's drink to that, shall we?'

Despite my offer of a bed in Ben's room for the night, Tom left a little after eleven. He'd only had a couple of glasses of wine, he reassured me, and plenty of coffee since, so I had no choice but to wave him off on the doorstep.

His mood as he left had been serious. Now I knew the truth I felt much less anxious about

Ffion, but Tom, on the other hand, felt much more so, because of Emily. Ffion rekindling old flames – even dead ones – was one thing, but the prospect of the man reclaiming Emily was another.

'But does he even *know* he has a daughter?' had been my first question on that point.

'Well, he *didn't*,' said Tom. 'At least, so Ffion said. But she could always tell him now!'

No wonder she'd been so upset to find out she was pregnant. Did she think he might leave her?

'And what about him? What was his situation?'

'A wife, two children.'

Were they still with him? And, more to the point, why did Ffion think he was dead if he wasn't?

'What do we do now?' I'd said as we'd parted.

He surprised me by bending to place a kiss on my cheek. 'Houston,' he said. 'I don't know. You tell me.'

CHAPTER ELEVEN

It HAD ALL FELT very dramatic on Monday night. But that was after three glasses of wine and a rather unsettling encounter with a man I was having to get to know all over again. Now it was Tuesday morning and raining, and the events all felt unreal. So the man my sister had had an affair with wasn't dead after all. There would be an explanation for it. And my little sister was thirty-seven, not thirteen. I understood the gravity of the situation for Tom, regarding Emily. But there did seem something wrong about interfering in the business of a grown woman, however much she had wanted my help in the past.

But Tom's anxiety was catching. However sane Ffion might be these days, she was still a volatile and impulsive person. If this man had the power to make her run to him after twelve long years, he might have the power to make her decide to tell him he had a daughter. And to persuade her to tell Emily too.

And I wasn't ruling out the possibility that she might then want to abandon her present life and simply try to pick up with him where she'd left off.

Tom called me a little after ten, from work, to ask if I'd heard anything. I had tried Ffion's mobile again, but only once, and reluctantly. This was Tom and Ffion's business now.

Yet hearing the stress in Tom's voice tugged at something in me.

'The number you've got,' he said. 'What area code was it?'

I went to fetch it and read it out to him. He knew it straight away.

'Swansea,' he said. That's a Swansea number. So that figures. If only we had a name.'

'Or the last two digits,' I said. 'There must be dozens of possibilities.'

'A hundred,' he said grimly.

'So what *is* there to do? Even if we trawled through all of them we might be none the wiser. And suppose we did manage to track him down, what purpose would it serve? It's Ffion we need to talk to – it's Ffion *you* need to talk to, Tom,' I said gently. 'I'm not sure it's up to me. I'm sure she'll get in touch when she's ready.' I was aware of his silence at the other end of the phone.

Then he sighed. 'I know. But you will let me know if you hear from her, won't you?'

'Of course I will,' I reassured him.

'Thanks,' he said. 'And thanks so much for last night, as well.'

'No thanks needed,' I told him. 'It was only a bowl of pasta.'

He laughed out loud. Then his voice became serious. 'Megan, I meant for your *company*.'

I put down the phone, feeling oddly frustrated. Something was stirring at the corner of my mind, but I couldn't figure out what. Swansea. It was something to do with Swansea. I was sure that it would come to me when it was good and ready. So, I launched myself into my notes on Romeo and Juliet instead.

But not for very long, because the phone started ringing. It wasn't Ffion, or Tom. It was a Mrs Pearson, whose name meant nothing to me, but who explained that she lived in the flat next to Ffion.

'I'm sorry to bother you,' she said, rather snootlily, 'but it's really not on.' She'd been given my number by Ffion, she told me, in case of emergencies. And this was one. She had to go out of town to look after an elderly relative. It was some seconds before I managed to work out why this should matter. Was there a leak perhaps?

'What's the problem, exactly?' I asked politely.

'Well, the dog, of course, lovely! I can't just leave him, can I? And to be honest, it's really not right anyway. I mean, it's all right for the odd night. We've been walking him three times a day and feeding him too, but a dog that size shouldn't be shut up in a flat day after day. It's not right.'

I agreed that it wasn't. Then I remembered Ffion mentioning the name Pearson, and the fact that her neighbour occasionally looked after Tigger when she was away overnight. 'Oh, dear,' I said. 'I had no idea. I assumed she'd taken him with her when she went.'

Which, now I thought about it, was unlikely. I waited then, hoping Mrs Pearson might shed light on where Ffion was. But she just pointed out that it would have been better if Ffion had put him in the kennels. Then she asked if I would be able to come up and sort him out. I agreed that I would, and, with my head still full of Shakespeare, I set off to Cardiff to take charge of the dog.

Mrs Pearson had already left when I got to Ffion's, but had left a note on the kitchen table to tell me she'd fed and walked the dog. I'd already decided I'd take Tigger home with me. If I had the dog it would ensure Ffion would have to get in touch sometime.

The flat was just as it had been when I'd left on Sunday, except for the neat row of dog food cans all rinsed out and standing on the worktop. I went into the study in the hope that there might be another message on the answer phone. But the light was an unblinking red dot on the machine.

I went into Ffion's bedroom.

'It's clear whose bed *you've* been sleeping on,' I scolded Tigger. I crossed the room to straighten the covers. Her dressing gown was lying at the end of the bed, similarly covered with hairs. Tigger's tail was thumping against my leg. He was clearly pleased at my unexpected arrival.

'Look at this!' I said, shaking it out. 'Don't get any ideas about making camp in *my* bedroom, OK?' And that was when it hit me. The dressing gown. I looked at it again. Of course! The dressing gown I was holding in my hands right now. *That* was the Swansea connection! I spread it on the bed. Old and threadbare as it was, it was still a very thick, very heavy, very expensive hotel dressing gown. I'd seen the crest on the breast pocket many times before. It read *Mariner's Wharf Hotel, Swansea*, embroidered in royal blue thread.

Long shots are not generally to be relied upon, but I knew my sister well. All at once I also knew that the chance of this shot hitting the target was actually very good indeed.

With Tigger click-clacking happily behind me, I strode back to the hallway and picked up the phone.

It took only a minute to confirm that Ffion was staying there, and only thirty seconds more to find out she wasn't in her room. So I left her a message, a short, rather curt one, telling her about her deserted dog. It would, I felt confident, ensure that she would ring me back.

That done, I pondered. Should I ring Tom and tell him? I wondered what exactly the hotel arrangements were. Was the man, Jack, staying there too? One thing was obvious. It explained why Ffion, who was these days so well-groomed, had such an attachment to a moth-eaten dressing gown that was more than ten years old.

I gathered up Tigger's bowl and blanket and thought some more. Perhaps I should wait before ringing Tom, until I'd spoken to Ffion at least. Though, herding the dog into the back of my car, it came to me grimly that the keeping of so many secrets hadn't helped anybody up to now.

It wasn't something I had to tussle with for long, however. I'd just got free of most of the late afternoon traffic and was heading out towards the motorway, when my mobile phone rang. I pulled off the dual carriageway into a side road.

But it was half a minute before I came to a halt and pulled the mobile from my handbag, and the ringing had stopped. I scrolled through the menu to find the missed calls. There was one word. Ffion. So she'd called me at last.

Relieved and irritated in equal measure, I pressed the button to return the call. It was answered straight away. But it wasn't Ffion's voice that was speaking.

'Is that Megan?' asked a female voice I didn't recognise. 'I'm sorry to trouble you but we weren't sure who to call, and –'

'Who is this?' I asked her, the hairs on my neck prickling.

'Oh, I'm sorry,' she said. 'I'm calling from the Mariner's Wharf Hotel. I'm afraid there's been an accident.'

CHAPTER TWELVE

MY MAIN THOUGHT, AS I headed down the motorway, was how very cross I was. It was one thing for my sister to go rushing off and causing everyone worry, quite another to get herself in such a state that she ended up in hospital. The girl on the phone had been helpful, but all she could tell me was that they'd found Ffion at the foot of the first floor stairs, passed out. They'd called an ambulance, and having found both her phone and my earlier message, had decided to call me. They suggested I head straight to the hospital.

I knew my anger was mostly anxiety, but I also knew a part of me really *was* angry with her. The leaden, lump-in-the-throat feeling was so familiar. Would there ever be a time when I *wouldn't* worry about my little sister? Would there ever be a time when I'd be allowed to let go?

The traffic was thicker now. It was almost five, and more cars were swarming on to the motorway with every junction we passed. Tigger, in the back of the car, was restless. If I didn't make better time, I would have to stop to let him out for a run. But then suddenly I was in Swansea. The sea was flat and granite grey as I swept past.

It didn't take long to reach the hospital – it was a place that I'd spent plenty of time visiting in the past – and within a few minutes I'd found out which ward she was on.

And found out, thank goodness, that she wasn't seriously hurt. She was sitting up in bed, flicking through a magazine, almost as if she hadn't a care in the world. Once I looked more closely, however, I could see that her face was blotched and her eyes were puffy. As if she'd been crying a great deal. Her eyes began to fill with tears even as I approached the bed. She rubbed the tears away with the back of her hand.

'They got hold of you then?' she said at once, fighting to regain her composure. 'I'm so sorry, Megan. I really didn't want to drag you all the way here. It was just stupid, stupid, stupid.'

She had, she told me, simply fallen down the stairs. Not a long flight of stairs, but enough that she had broken a bone in her foot. She'd been X-rayed and was now waiting to have her plaster put on. She was also, she told me, concussed. Which was why the hotel had insisted on calling the ambulance, and why they were keeping her in hospital overnight.

I threw my jacket down on one of the chairs by the bed but I didn't sit on it myself. I felt I'd been sitting in the car half the day. The morning suddenly seemed a lifetime ago.

'How on earth did it happen?' I asked, nodding towards her foot, and trying but failing to keep irritation out of my voice.

'I don't know, really I don't,' she said, apologetically. 'I just passed out. One minute I was at the top of the stairs and the next I found myself at the bottom.' She threw the magazine down to join my jacket. 'Actually, I'm not being honest, Megan. I haven't been eating. I haven't been sleeping. I've just been –'

'Been *what*, exactly? Tom and I have been tearing our hair out, and –'

'Tom?' She looked really shocked. '*Tom* knows I'm here?'

'No, but he certainly knows *why* you're here, Ffion.' I sat down now, feeling suddenly weary. 'And so do I,' I added heavily. 'He told me.'

Tears shone in her eyes again and then overflowed, tracking in twin streams down her cheeks and dripping on to the hospital robe.

CHAPTER THIRTEEN

IT HADN'T, SHE SAID, been a casual affair. Nothing like that. From the moment she and Jack had met they'd simply known they had to be together. And though Ffion was talking in a language that seemed more like romantic fiction than the business of real life infidelity, I could see she meant every word she said.

Tom had been right. Ffion and Jack had met when she'd been working on the hospital project here in Swansea. Jack was a young doctor, only recently qualified, and, like Ffion, he was already married. Unlike her, however, he was already a parent as well. He had two small children, one barely out of nappies. They'd tried all the usual things such as not seeing each other, trying to make a go of their marriages, telling themselves they'd get over it. They'd ended it, in fact, more than once.

But nothing worked, and the affair had continued. Neither of them was able to do without the other, though both of them – particularly Jack – were racked by guilt. But then Ffion had found out she was pregnant with Emily, and doing nothing was no longer an option. She'd agonised about whether to tell him. Whatever the fate of her own unhappy marriage, this was a man who already had children. How could she take their father away from them? She'd still been wrestling with her decision when she found out he'd been killed.

Only he hadn't.

I thrust the tissue box at her. 'But how on earth could you *make* a mistake like that?'

Ffion pulled at the bed sheet. 'I still can't believe it,' she said. 'The first I knew of it was days after the accident. I was used to not being able to get hold of him, of course.' She looked grimly at me. 'That's how affairs are. But when almost a week passed, I began to worry. Had his wife found out about us? Did he want to end things? I didn't know what to think. So I rang the hospital he worked at by then, in Carmarthen, and they told me he'd been in an accident and would be in hospital for some time. I didn't know what to do. I couldn't call his home, could I? So in the end I decided I would go there myself. But when I got there it was awful. There was this big relatives' room – I could see it just off the entrance. His wife was in there, and all sorts of other people.' She plucked another tissue from the box.

'So I panicked. I just left. And the next day I rang instead, pretending to be a relative. And then they told me he'd died the previous night.'

'And that was that?'

'That was that.' Her voice was flat. 'I was three months pregnant and the man I loved was dead. But I was *wrong*,' she whispered. 'If only I'd known. You can't imagine the thoughts I've been living with for the past few days, Megan. I was *wrong*.'

I was as confused as ever. 'But *how* were you wrong? How could anyone get something like that *wrong*?'

Her answering smile was entirely without humour. She stared into the middle distance. Not really talking to me at all.

'If I'd just glanced at a newspaper I would have known the truth. If I'd known he'd been with Jack –'

'Known *who* had been with Jack?'

She looked at me as if I hadn't been listening. 'His father, of course!'

'His *father*?'

She nodded, gulping back more tears. 'When I rang the hospital – I – I just asked how Dr Williams was. If I'd used his full name –'

'But you *did*.'

73

'No, you don't get it. His father had been in the *car* with him. And he was a doctor as well. It was *him* that was lying there in Intensive Care, the day before, dying!'

I was trying to make sense of it. 'But surely they would have asked *which* Dr Williams. Surely they would –'

She was shaking her head violently. 'That's just it. They wouldn't have! Because Jack wasn't even a patient there! He'd been taken straight to a specialist hospital in London after the accident. He had bad head injuries. He was in there for months. And all that time...'

She turned to look at me now, but without really seeing. 'I saw his wife, you know. A few weeks later. She was pushing a buggy. I nearly went up to her, Megan. I *so* nearly went up to her. Not to tell her who I was or anything, but just to tell her I'd known her husband and that I was sorry. But I *didn't*. If I had, then perhaps I would have found out...'

She tailed off, too tearful to continue. I kept having to remind myself that these were all things she'd only just found out herself. The shock must have been huge.

'But it doesn't make sense. Why didn't he try to get in touch with you?'

She wiped her eyes. 'Because I hadn't tried to contact *him*. He thought...' She sniffed. 'He thought *I'd* decided to end things. Plus he had no idea when he'd be able to work again – didn't know how he'd be able to support his wife and children, let alone leave them for me. He felt he'd have nothing to give me but...' She paused to gulp back a fresh flood of tears. I tried to imagine what hearing this all these years on must have felt like. I couldn't begin. She had paid an awful price for her infidelity. 'He tried,' she finished. 'A few years back, after his divorce, he tried to find me. But by that time we'd moved to Cardiff with Tom's work, and...' She spread her hands in front of her, now unable to speak.

'And now you've seen him again,' I said gently. 'So what next?'

She looked into the distance for a long moment, then turned back to me. 'I'm so sorry I never told you, Megan. Truly I am. I nearly did, so many times. I just didn't know what to do. Should I keep the baby? Should I tell Tom the truth?' Her voice was a whisper. She pinched her thumb and finger together. 'I was *this* close to ending it all...but I had a baby to think of. That was all that kept me going. And Tom...well, he knew nothing. And he was so excited about Emily, Megan. It would have been too cruel, too awful. And for what? What good would it have done to break his heart? So in the end I decided...well...' She brushed at the robe, agitated. 'You know what I decided. Only now Jack's found me, and...well, how do you *deal* with something like this?'

I had no answer for her. I didn't know.

'And him – Jack – what does *he* say? What does *he* want?'

'He wanted to see me,' she said simply. 'He found me and he wanted to see me, and now... well, there's Emily...' She seemed to drift away into thought. 'He saw my picture, you know. That's how he found me. The picture in that magazine last month. I showed it to you – the one from Scott's book-launch party.' I nodded. 'He rang work, pretended he was a journalist, and got my phone numbers.' She had a faraway look in her eyes, as if bemused by fate's hand in things. 'Who would have thought it?'

'But what *now*?' I said again.

She shook her head. 'Oh, Megan, I wish he'd never found me. I'm so churned up. I love Scott, I *do*... but...oh, I wish I didn't have to deal with all this.'

She stopped and glanced behind me. I turned to see a nurse approaching the bed with a wheelchair.

'Time for my plaster,' said Ffion, wiping her eyes with the last of her tissue. She leant across and squeezed my arm. 'Thank you,' she said. 'I can't tell you how much it means to be able to tell you the truth. I've been living with secrets for so long.'

CHAPTER FOURTEEN

As FFION WAS GOING to be some time, I decided to go and deal with Tigger. Though I'd given him a quick run when we arrived at the hospital, he'd been shut up again for nearly an hour. Perhaps I'd drive down to the front and go for a walk on the beach. And call Tom, maybe. There wasn't much to tell him until I'd spoken further to Ffion, but at least I could let him know I'd found her. I made my way across to the corner of the hospital car park. It would put his mind at rest, on that score at least. But then, would it? Wouldn't he want to come rushing down to confront her?

No, I decided. I shouldn't ring Tom yet. It would be sensible to wait until I'd spoken more to her. Yet I wished I *did* have a reason to call him. He was in my mind, of course, what with Ffion and Emily. I put my key in the lock to let Tigger out. He was in my mind, full stop, I realised.

What was I going to do now? It seemed pointless to drive home only to have to come back again tomorrow, but I had Tigger to think of. What on earth would I do with him if I stayed? I had a brainwave and rang the hotel receptionist.

'Oh, you can leave him here, no problem,' she told me. 'Lots of our guests like to bring their pets on holiday. People with pets tend to holiday in this country, rather than abroad, don't they?'

She was chatty and helpful, and probably, I guessed, a little relieved that nothing more serious had happened to one of their guests. So I would stay. Ffion's room had been booked for tonight. I could drive Ffion back to Cardiff in the morning. With her ankle in plaster she would have to leave her own car here for now.

At the hotel I showered and had a sandwich. Then I left Tigger in the willing hands of the receptionist, and drove back to the hospital a little after eight.

Ffion was looking more composed now.

'So,' I said, as soon as I'd sat down. She wasn't in bed, but in the armchair beside it. Her foot was encased in plaster and resting on a low stool. 'What happened? You met him?'

Ffion nodded. 'I came down here Sunday night. We talked. He's divorced now. His children are teenagers.'

A sudden thought occurred to me. 'Is he staying at the hotel as well?'

She shook her head. 'No. And he doesn't know I am. I didn't make a plan, Megan. I just knew I needed to get away. Get *here*. I couldn't face Scott until I'd sorted things in my head. So I just threw some things in a bag and booked in at the Mariner's Wharf. It was the hotel we used to –'

'I know. I worked that much out.'

She managed a wry grin. 'I was in such a state by then I didn't know what I was doing. I just thought I'd come here. It was lucky they had a room. I thought I would meet him, and…well, take it from there. You don't have a plan for these things, Megan. I didn't know how I'd feel. Only that I had to see him. That if I didn't see him…well. It's been a long time. An awful lot of "what ifs" and "if onlys". '

'And have you seen him again, since?' She shook her head. 'So what *have* you been doing? Apart from not eating and not sleeping, that is.'

'Thinking,' she said simply. 'Thinking about what was the right thing to do.'

She was talking as if there was definitely a decision to be made. Tom had been right.

80

Telling Jack about Emily now *was* an option. And was leaving Scott an option too? For a ghost?

'What about Emily?' I asked her. 'And what about *his* children? Where do they figure in all this?'

She must have caught an edge in my voice, because her own was suddenly short.

'You really think I haven't *thought* about that? About Emily, and Tom, and what this would do to them? What right have I got to turn their lives upside down?' She was echoing my own thoughts, so I didn't answer but simply nodded, relieved.

Though not for long. 'But *Jack* has rights too, Megan,' she said hotly. 'He's Emily's father. And he's –'

'But are you sure of that? *Absolutely* sure? I mean, if Tom had reason to believe she was his, then...well, how *can* you be so sure?'

Ffion shook her head sadly. 'You don't realise. There's no question. Tom couldn't *have* children. We'd both had tests. He'd already been told –' She tailed off. I was aghast. More bombshells. It was as if I was talking to a stranger. But she seemed to read my thoughts. 'We didn't tell *any*one, Megan. Not a soul.'

It was all in the past, I reminded myself. 'But if that were so, how could he have thought Em was his?'

'You always hope,' she said quietly. 'Miracles do happen. It wasn't difficult for him to believe it, Megan. He so desperately wanted it to be so. So I – well, it was easy for me to –'

This prompted a fresh bout of tears. 'I shouldn't have told Tom the truth. Why did I tell him? It was just that as soon as Em was born...' she sniffed. '...Every day she grew more like Jack. If you saw him – Jack *is* her father, Megan. What right do I have to keep it from him?'

I grabbed her wrist with my hand. 'Every right! Look, this isn't even *about* rights, Ffion. This is about what's best for Emily. Surely you can see that? Doesn't *he* understand that? What does he have to say? Surely he doesn't expect to simply walk into her life and replace Tom as her father!'

Ffion was shaking her head.

'He doesn't,' she said softly. 'And he won't be.'

'So he *does* understand? He doesn't expect you to tell Emily about him?'

'He doesn't expect anything,' she said. 'Because he doesn't know. All those lies. So many lies. Is there ever going to be an end to them?' A single tear rolled down her cheek and she brushed it away. 'Don't worry. I didn't tell him about Emily.'

CHAPTER FIFTEEN

THERE DIDN'T SEEM MUCH to be done, except to dry Ffion's tears. I had been wrong. I needn't have worried. My sister had already made her decision. And acted on it. She wouldn't be seeing Jack again. She'd come here, she told me, not with any thoughts of their future. Just of their past. Of what might have been and now never would. She'd come down to see him already knowing that her future was with Scott. But also knowing that fate had given her a chance to close the circle, at last. And to say a proper goodbye.

'That's it, then, is it?' asked Tom when I called him from the hotel late in the evening. I could tell by his voice he'd thought of little else. He didn't sound convinced. He'd been haunted by Jack's ghost for almost all of Emily's life.

'That's it,' I told him firmly. I believed it. In our own ways, we'd both got things wrong about my sister. We'd made assumptions about her that were no longer sound. 'She never intended telling him anything about Emily,' I said. 'She just wanted to lay the ghost to rest. That was all.'

They'd need to talk, of course. I knew Tom wouldn't feel entirely comfortable until he'd had a chance to discuss things with Ffion himself. And perhaps, one day, they *would* decide to tell Emily. I hoped not. But that was their business. I was only glad to be able to put it out of my mind. I felt strangely liberated. But there was little else to be said to Tom. Which made me feel suddenly sad. I wondered how long it would be before our paths crossed again.

'Well,' I began. 'I guess I'd better get to bed.'

'And how about *you*?' he said suddenly. 'Are you OK? You must be shattered.'

'I'm fine,' I told him, touched by his concern. 'I'm staying down here tonight and taking Ffion home in the morning. Then I really must get back to my school work.'

I said goodbye to Tom and put down the phone.

'Houston?' Tom said. 'We have a problem.'

It was late the following Friday afternoon. The last day of the school holidays, and my last chance to get to grips with my neglected autumn teaching plan. Which, despite the temptation of the sunshine outside, was what I'd been doing when Tom called. He was "out west" as he called it, having been to a meeting with a client in Tenby. Did I have anything on other than Shakespeare? If not, he wondered if I fancied an hour or two off. Trailing up the M4 at tea time on a Friday was the last thing he fancied doing, so he thought he'd stop for supper. There was a little pub he'd been told about, in Laugharne. It wasn't too far from where I lived.

And here we were now, in his car. Just some fresh air and sunshine, I'd told myself sternly. That was all. That and an excuse to escape work for a while. Even so, I'd hastily changed out of my jeans and T shirt, and was sitting beside him now in my best summer dress.

I glanced across at him, feeling butterflies in my stomach. All too aware that he kept looking at me as he drove. 'A problem?' I asked him, now feeling anxious. Had something new happened with Ffion?

I could see a smile forming at the edge of his mouth. 'Well, it's not really *your* problem. It's just that...'

'Yes?'

His smile widened. 'Remember what I said to you about being wary of getting involved?' I nodded. 'And how you said you knew how I felt?'

I nodded again. The car slowed as we approached the pub car park. The building itself was decorated with baskets of flowers, heavy with late summer blooms. He pulled on the handbrake and turned to look at me. I could feel a blush creep across my cheeks. Crazy. But real. And probably matching my lipstick. Me! In lipstick? He was looking at me intently now.

'I've decided that being wary isn't always the best policy. Being wary might just be my undoing.'

I held his gaze as I undid my seat belt. 'How so?'

'Because we've met up again after, what – seven years?' I nodded. 'And me being the way I am, chances are that unless I do something about it, it could be another seven years before we *next* meet. Emily's eighteenth birthday party, most probably. Which means –' he grinned again. 'That we'll both be none the wiser.'

I blinked at him. 'None the wiser about what?'

He undid his own seat belt and twisted to face me. 'About this.'

'This?'

He pulled the keys from the ignition. 'About me and you,' he said softly. He looked shy himself now. Hesitant. Embarrassed.

I swallowed. 'Us?'

He looked bashful. 'Well, *me*, at any rate. I don't know if there's an "us" yet. It's just that since seeing you again, Megan, I've been thinking.'

Was I hearing him right? My pulse raced. 'Thinking what?'

He took a breath. 'Thinking that if I don't do something quick, we'll never know, will we?'

'Know what?'

'Know whether it would work out between us.'

His eyes shone. The same twinkle he'd always had in his eye, undimmed by the passing of the years. Tom? Tom and *me*? Putting the thought into words felt scary. It wasn't just Ffion and her problems I had had to let go of, I realised. I had all sorts of baggage of my own to lose as well. The fall-out from a failed marriage. My reluctance to trust a man again. But *this* man?

I returned his gaze now, conscious of a heat growing in my stomach. I'd always thought

Tom was attractive. He *was*. But he'd been my sister's husband, so it hadn't even registered. And once things went wrong, I had almost despised him.

For so long. So many years. But I'd been wrong. And one thing was clear. I'd been thinking as well. Since seeing him again, I'd been thinking *about* him. He'd barely been out of my thoughts. And here he was telling me the feeling was mutual. *Could* this work out?

Sitting there looking into Tom's eyes, my heart told me I'd just have to risk it. I couldn't keep it chained up forever. We got out of the car and I waited while he locked it, my heart thumping wildly.

He walked round to join me. Though he now looked less certain, and anxious for my answer, he held out his hand, waiting for mine.

Slipping my hand into his felt as natural as breathing. I squeezed it, feeling suddenly light-headed. Even more so as he turned and put his other arm around me.

'It may not work out,' I said, as he dipped his head to kiss me.

His mouth was close to mine now. 'But you're willing to risk it?'

Ffion's secret had caused all sorts of heartache, but something else too. A re-awakening of my heart.

My kiss answered for me.

THE CORPSE'S TALE

BY KATHERINE JOHN

Dai Morgan has the body of a man and the mind of a child. He lived with his mother in the Mid Wales village of Llan, next door to bright, beautiful 19 year old Anna Harris. The vicar found Anna's naked, battered body in the churchyard one morning. The police discovered Anna's bloodstained earring in Dai's pocket.

The judge gave Dai life.

After ten years in gaol Dai appealed against his sentence and was freed. Sergeants Trevor Joseph and Peter Collins are sent to Llan to reopen the case. But the villagers refuse to believe Dai innocent. The Llan police do not make mistakes or allow murderers to walk free.

Do they?

KATHERINE JOHN is the author of four crime novels and also writes as Catrin Collier for Orion. She lives with her family near Swansea, Wales.

ISBN 1905170319
price £2.99